Table of Contents

The Night of a Thousand Lanterns

A Lesson of Release

(A Crimson Alliance Micro-Tale)

Acknowledgements

The Night of a Thousand Lanterns exist because stories do not form in isolation.

To those who have followed the Crimson Alliance Universe (a.k.a., CAU) from its earliest stories, thank you for trusting these characters across worlds, conflicts, and moments of quiet reflection. Your willingness to walk with them through both battle and stillness continues to shape how these stories are told.

To new readers, welcome. This tale was written to stand on its own, but it also carries the weight of journeys already taken. If this story invites you to explore further, then it has done its work.

This story is also a reflection on tradition, healing, and the importance of choosing when to let go and when to carry something forward. For that, I acknowledge the cultures and rituals that inspired this narrative, not as replicas, but as sources of respect and reflection.

Finally, thank you to those who encourage modern storytelling, evolving tools, and thoughtful revision. Stories improve when they are allowed to grow.

~ **K.A. Dunlap**

The Night of a Thousand Lanterns

A Lesson of Release

K.A. Dunlap

(A Crimson Alliance Micro-Tale)

The Night of a Thousand Lanterns: A Lesson of Release

ISBN:

Paperback: 979-8-9929819-9-5

Cover Design by Nh Arafat

Interior Formatting by Amna Jehangir

Contact the Author

KADunlap@TheCAU.net

Website: https://www.TheCAU.net

Published by: Kevin A. Dunlap, LLC

First Edition

Character Premise

The following characters have shared battles and journeys before, but no prior knowledge is required to meet them here. This story stands on its own.

Kimiko

Kimiko is a disciplined warrior trained in both ninja and samurai traditions, grounded in restraint, observation, and precision. Raised in a culture where mastery is measured not by dominance but by control, she learned early that silence can be as powerful as action. Though she has fought across worlds and survived conflicts far beyond her home, Kimiko remains deeply shaped by the rituals and teachings of her childhood. Her strength lies not only in her skill with blades, but in her ability to read spaces, people, and intentions. Returning to her homeland is not a retreat. It is an act of reconnection. For Kimiko, ritual is not nostalgia. It is how meaning is preserved.

Freija

Freija is the younger twin princess and a warrior of Icelandia, a world defined by cold skies, open horizons, and endurance. Despite her small 5'2" frame, she possesses natural, winged flight and heightened perception, her wings as integral to her balance and awareness as her strength. She serves as both protector and sentinel, often sensing danger before it fully forms. Though her power is unmistakable, Freija carries it with quiet confidence rather than display. She values loyalty, shared purpose, and the bonds forged through trust. In unfamiliar worlds, she observes carefully, honoring traditions that are not her own while standing ready to defend those she calls family.

Adrian Flynn

Adrian is a human born on a distant Earth-settled colony, and a natural star pilot whose survival depends on preparation, adaptability, and timing. He is neither the strongest nor the most imposing presence in a room, but he understands logistics, movement, and consequences better than most. His humor serves as a pressure valve, masking a mind that is always calculating distance, risk, and contingency. Among warriors and legends, Adrian's role is grounding. He ensures that plans end with everyone still standing, and that journeys, no matter how strange, have their way home. He stays not because he must, but because these are the people he chooses.

Prelude

In August 2318, shortly after a great conflict, the seven members of the Crimson Alliance did not remain together. Recovery took different forms for each of them.

Adrian and Grilka stepped away from the aftermath on a distant pleasure world, allowing time and routine to dull the sharp edges left behind.

Kimiko, meanwhile, accepted Freija's invitation to come to Icelandia, a distant ice-world where winged sentients ruled the skies and cold horizons demanded discipline as much as strength.

Those weeks passed as they needed to.

Then Freija reached out to Adrian with a request. Not for aid. Not for urgency. Simply to come to Icelandia, because Kimiko had something she wished to share.

Chapter 1:
The Invite

The Pickup

Adrian set his small two-seater ship, the *Starlight Shadow,* down on the landing pad just outside of Frostholm, the capital of the ice world of Icelandia. He stepped off the ramp into a blast of cutting wind.

Adrian Flynn

The cold struck immediately, sharper than anything he had known on Earth. Thinner, too, as if the planet itself had been engineered without consideration for visitors.

Fantastic, he thought. *Five seconds on the ground and I already miss the vacuum of space.*

THE NIGHT OF A THOUSAND LANTERNS: A LESSON OF RELEASE

His breath fogged at once, dissolving into the air almost as quickly as it formed. He pulled his jacket tighter and took in the ice-bright horizon in silence.

A shadow crossed the platform from above, followed by the soft thunder of displaced air. Freija descended, her turquoise wings catching the light as she dropped through the cold sky. She landed with practiced ease, boots settling into the frost without slipping. Her wings folded neatly against her back, her posture balanced and deliberate.

Freija

"Your timing is precise," she said, her smile warm but controlled. "The winds are calm... for now."

"That's what every dangerous planet says," Adrian replied, "right before it proves a point."

Freija did not wait for another word. She closed the distance in two quick steps and wrapped her arms around him in a fierce, unapologetic hug.

Adrian froze for half a heartbeat, then laughed softly and returned it. "Good to see you too."

She held the embrace for another couple of heartbeats before stepping back, a broad, unguarded smile on her face.

"Come with me," Freija said. "I want to show you something."

Near the tallest spire stood Kimiko. She wore a winter parka suited for Icelandia's cold, the twin katana hilts rising over her shoulders. The blades were secured with care, not displayed, as if they were simply another part of her silhouette. She remained still as they approached, gaze steady, already aware of them long before they closed the distance.

There was a subtle absence of tension in her posture. Her shoulders rested naturally, her stance unforced, as if the cold no longer demanded her full attention.

"Adrian," Kimiko said, inclining her head in greeting.

He returned the bow, hands still buried in his jacket pockets. "Kimiko. You look... comfortable. Which feels unfair, given the temperature."

The faintest curve touched her lips, not quite a smile, but close enough to acknowledge the attempt.

Freija closed the distance quickly, taking Adrian by the arm and urging him forward.

"Kimiko has news," she said, eyes bright. "Important news."

Kimiko exhaled once, slow and controlled, and cast Freija a sidelong look that carried more patience than reprimand. "I was about to tell him."

Freija lifted her hands in surrender, unapologetic. Kimiko turned to Adrian, her tone softening.

"My hometown of Tatsumi, just outside of Kyoto, holds a traditional annual festival in mid-August. I have not attended in many years. It is called Tōrō Nagashi, or the Night of a Thousand Lanterns."

Freija nodded once, approval clear. "It sounds beautiful."

"It is," Kimiko said. For a brief moment her gaze shifted... not softer exactly, but distant in the way memory can pull. "I have not seen it since I left home." She paused, choosing each word with care. "After everything that happened on Icelandia over the last month, I thought it would be good to visit my hometown again. With friends."

Kimiko

Adrian blinked, caught off guard. Kimiko didn't often use the *F-word.*

"Well," he said, keeping his voice even, "when a highly trained ninja invites you to a lantern festival, I've learned it's best to accept."

Kimiko met his gaze without flinching. "Only if you arrive on time."

Freija's mouth twitched, and a quiet laugh slipped out as she shook her head.

Boarding the Starlight Shadow

The Starlight Shadow sat parked on the ice plateau like an impatient metallic bird, a small cargo ship meant for light hauls and fast interstellar travel, built for speed rather than comfort. Its engines starting venting steam into Icelandia's frigid air. Ice and stone stretched to the horizon beneath a pale sky that felt too sharp to belong anywhere else. Adrian led the way up the ramp.

"As a reminder," he said, glancing back at the two warrior women, "this ship sleeps two and the cockpit only fits the same number of actual seats. One of you will either stand or sit in the small lounge."

Freija's attention sharpened the moment they stepped aboard. "May I sit in the cockpit first? I want to see Icelandia from space again."

"Of course," Adrian said. "Just try not to press anything that glows, hums, clicks, vibrates, or looks important."

"That appears to be everything," Freija observed.

"Yes," Adrian replied. "It is."

Inside the cockpit, Freija moved carefully, folding her wings closer as she leaned forward to study the partially familiar controls. Through the forward canopy, the ice plateau remained fixed beneath them. Adrian slid into the pilot's chair on the left while Freija eased into the co-pilot's seat beside him, her attention already drawn outward rather than inward.

Kimiko stepped in behind them, taking up a steady position near the doorway. She assessed the space in silence, noting distances and lines of movement rather than the displays.

"Living area is back there if you want to strap in," Adrian said, nodding over his shoulder.

Kimiko glanced briefly toward the corridor, then shook her head. "Standing is fine."

Adrian nodded once. "Keep your footing when we lift then."

The engines hummed more loudly as the Starlight Shadow powered up. Ice and rock slid away beneath them as the ship lifted smoothly from the plateau. The sky darkened gradually, blue fading into black as altitude increased. Freija leaned forward slightly, her gaze fixed on the widening curve below.

Icelandia spread out beneath them now. A world of frozen continents and pale light, whole and distant all at once.

Freija fell quiet. Her hands rested loosely against the edge of the console as she took in the sight, wings held still. For a moment, she did not speak, simply watched as her planet slipped farther away.

"It never looks the same from above," she said at last, her voice softer than before.

Adrian did not look at her. "That usually means it mattered."

Kimiko glanced toward the canopy, then back to Freija. She said nothing, but her presence shifted subtly, attentive without intrusion. Freija met moments like this openly, without hesitation. It was a freedom Kimiko rarely permitted herself, and one she admired all the same.

The last traces of atmosphere vanished. Stars sharpened ahead.

"This should be an interesting journey," Kimiko said.

"Oh, guaranteed," Adrian replied as his hands moved across the controls. "You invited us, after all. You knew what you were signing up for."

Kimiko exhaled, not quite a laugh, but close. "I did."

Moments later, space folded inward. Light stretched into clean lines as the Starlight Shadow slipped into hyperspace, leaving Icelandia behind.

Lanterns of Home

A few hours later, the streaking starlight had returned to mere pinpoints. Earth filled the forward canopy in gradual detail. Adrian pointed the ship toward Japan.

From their western approach, the Sea of Japan stretched beneath the Starlight Shadow, its surface darkening as the last traces of sunlight slipped away. The water reflected a fading band of gold near the horizon, thinning as the ship continued eastward. Adrian eased the craft lower, flight controls steady, descent smooth and unhurried.

Dusk had already begun to settle.

The main island of Honshu emerged ahead; its coastline defined by shadowed ridges and the first pinpricks of evening light. The farther east they traveled, the deeper the sky became. Blue replaced amber. Then indigo. Cities began to glow, not all at once, but gradually, as if waking rather than announcing themselves.

Kimiko sat in the co-pilot's seat, posture straight, hands resting loosely near the console. She wore light summer clothing now, appropriate for August, her katanas secured across her back with familiar precision. She watched the land below without speaking.

Behind her, Freija leaned forward, wings folded close, eyes fixed on the world unfolding beneath them. The glow from the cities reflected softly across her features, warmer than the cold light of Icelandia. She did not try to hide her awe.

"It feels whole," Freija said quietly. "Like it remembers itself."

Kimiko nodded once. "It does."

Clouds thinned as the ship descended. Rivers caught the last remaining light, silver threads winding through valleys already surrendering to night. Kyoto appeared ahead, not bright, but steady. Lanterns were being lit across the city, one by one, spreading outward in patient clusters.

Adrian adjusted their approach vector. "Tatsumi perimeter in sight. Clearance confirmed."

The Starlight Shadow angled slightly east, engines lowering in tone as forested land rose to meet them. Smaller settlements marked themselves with scattered lights, subdued and calm, preparing rather than celebrating.

Kimiko's breathing slowed. Not from tension, but from focus.

"I have not returned here in many years," she said at last. "Thank you. Both of you."

Freija inclined her head. Adrian kept his eyes on the approach, voice steady. "Then let's land properly."

The ship descended toward the waiting lights below.

Tatsumi.

The village was awake, but restrained, as if holding itself just short of ceremony.

Kimiko stepped down the ramp first. She paused at the base, drawing in a slow breath. Cedar. Incense. Smoke carried low on warm evening air.

"This scent," she said quietly. "I remember it."

Freija joined her, voice respectful. "This is where you began."

Kimiko nodded. "Yes."

Lanterns lined the paths ahead, their paper shells glowing softly, casting warm pools of light across stone and packed earth. The village moved with deliberate care. Villagers adjusted cords, set offerings, spoke in low voices. Children carried folded lanterns, still unlit, their excitement contained by the hour.

Adrian descended last, leaving his jacket draped over the pilot's seat. His hands rested in his pockets as he took in the narrow paths, the careful spacing of light, the sense of preparation rather than display.

Kimiko gestured for them to follow.

THE NIGHT OF A THOUSAND LANTERNS: A LESSON OF RELEASE

They walked deeper into Tatsumi as twilight gave way to night. A shrine drum sounded somewhere ahead, slow and measured, marking time rather than calling attention.

Freija glanced toward the river where lanterns waited along the bank, folded and ready. "They will be released tomorrow."

"Yes," Kimiko replied. "As they always are."

She slowed near the water and lifted one of the lanterns, holding it gently, studying the paper surface in silence.

"Tomorrow," she said softly. "I will see you again."

She set the lantern back among the others.

For now, that was enough.

Chapter 2:
The Blessing Ceremony

Enter the Master

The festival plaza was quieter than it would be tomorrow.

Lanterns already hung from the bamboo arches that framed the clearing, their paper bodies pale and unlit, stirring gently in the warm evening breeze. The sun had dipped low enough to soften the light, casting long shadows across the packed earth and polished stone paths. Villagers moved through the space with care, adjusting cords, aligning offerings, preparing rather than celebrating.

This was not the public hour. This was the hour of readiness.

Kimiko slowed as they reached the edge of the plaza. Without conscious effort, her posture straightened, her steps becoming more measured. Memory guided her now, not hesitation.

At the center of the clearing stood a raised wooden platform, worn smooth by generations of bare feet and patient hands. Its surface bore no ornament beyond age and care. The space around it remained deliberately open, as if nothing else was meant to compete with what would occur there.

The first to enter were six figures dressed in clean, simple robes, their movements synchronized but not rehearsed.

Kimiko turned slightly toward Freija and Adrian. "Those are the initiates," she said quietly. "They stand at the beginning of their spiritual path. They represent new beginnings."

The initiates moved into the plaza with measured, deliberate steps. They positioned themselves along the outer edges of the clearing and near the lantern frames, hands folded, eyes lowered. Their role was not to lead, but to prepare. To observe. To hold the space steady.

A moment later, four more figures entered.

Fewer in number, they wore similar robes, distinguished only by ceremonial sashes draped across their shoulders. The fabric of each sash showed subtle signs of wear. These were not decorations. They were earned.

Freija leaned closer, her voice barely above a whisper. "Who are they?"

"The adepts," Kimiko replied. "They have walked this path for many years. They train others, preserve the rites, and support the Master."

Freija hesitated, then asked gently, "Were you ever one of them?"

Kimiko shook her head once. "No. At that time, my father was still training me. The honor code of the samurai. The discipline of the ninja." Her voice remained even, but there was no distance in it. Only truth.

Freija studied her friend for a moment, warmth flickering in her eyes.

The adepts moved closer to the platform, positioning themselves with practiced ease. They stood ready to assist, never to command.

Master Shigenori

Only then did the plaza fall completely still.

An elderly man stepped onto the platform.

Time had thinned his frame but not his presence. His back remained straight, his movements deliberate and exact. He wore layered ceremonial robes in muted tones, carefully maintained, their simplicity speaking of continuity rather than status. In one hand, he carried a polished staff, its surface marked by years of steady use.

No announcement was made.

None was needed.

Kimiko inhaled quietly.

"That is Master Shigenori," she said. "He taught me the Lantern Rite when I was still very young."

Freija inclined her head at once, wings folding closer to her back. Adrian followed, bowing with the same instinctive respect shown by the villagers nearby. No one had instructed them. The Master's presence required it.

Master Shigenori surveyed the plaza, his gaze calm, unhurried. When he spoke, it was in low, measured Japanese, his voice steady and warm, meant for those close enough to listen rather than for a crowd.

Kimiko translated softly. "He is blessing the lanterns before nightfall. Asking for clarity. For guidance. For those who will be honored tomorrow."

At a subtle gesture from the Master, one of the initiates stepped forward. He moved carefully, as if aware of every eye upon him, and lifted a lantern larger than the others.

The lantern's paper was etched with ancient kanji, worn smooth by repetition and care. Master Shigenori accepted it with both hands, neither hurried nor hesitant, and placed it upon a carved pedestal at the front of the platform.

Then the initiate retreated to his position, shoulders squared, breath carefully measured.

Freija leaned closer, her voice respectful. "He handles it like a living thing."

"It represents all those who carried the rite before him," Kimiko replied. "Masters. Teachers. Guardians of memory. This ritual is centuries old."

The plaza fell into stillness.

No drums sounded. No music marked the moment. This was not performance. This was preparation.

Master Shigenori rested both hands upon his staff and continued the blessing, his words flowing evenly as the lanterns waited above them, unlit and patient. Around the clearing, villagers stood quietly, holding the space together through shared understanding.

Kimiko felt the moment settle deeply. Not as nostalgia, but as continuity.

Freija stood just behind her, wings folded neatly, offering presence rather than vigilance. The rite asked nothing more.

Adrian remained still, hands at his sides, eyes moving slowly across the plaza. Not searching. Not measuring. Simply observing a place that understood the value of waiting.

Above them, the lanterns swayed gently in the evening air.

Tomorrow, they would be released. Tonight, they were being prepared.

Lantern Walk

Non-ceremonial lantern light shifted from ivory to amber to muted red as they passed beneath them, each glow distinct, none competing for attention. Paper shells swayed gently overhead, casting warm pools of light across stone and packed earth. Shadows stretched and softened with every step, moving slowly, as if the village itself walked beside them.

Kimiko moved at the center, her pace unhurried. Her summer kimono whispered faintly against her steps, a sound she had not realized she missed until it returned. She did not speak. She did not need to. The lantern light traced familiar paths beneath her feet, illuminating memory without pressing it forward.

Freija walked just behind her, wings folded close, careful not to disturb the cords above. Her gaze moved between the lanterns and the narrow street ahead, taking in the rhythm rather than the detail.

"This place feels different from Icelandia," she said quietly. "Not weaker. Just... inviting."

Kimiko inclined her head. "It carries remembrance instead of vigilance."

Adrian exhaled softly, hands in his pockets as he looked upward. The lanterns reflected faintly in his eyes.

"I'll admit," he said, "a year ago I didn't think my life would include fighting alongside demons, princesses, ninjas, ancient rituals... or walking under glowing paper lights."

Freija glanced at him, the corner of her mouth lifting. "You sound disappointed."

"No," Adrian replied. "Just recalibrating expectations."

Kimiko allowed a faint smile. Brief. Genuine.

"You adapted quickly," she said.

"Adaptable," Adrian answered lightly. "Also helps when your companions are terrifyingly competent."

They continued on in silence, lanterns swaying gently above. Somewhere beyond the trees, water moved along the riverbank, unseen but present, its sound threading through the quiet.

After a moment, Freija spoke again. "This past year," she said thoughtfully, "it changed all of us."

Kimiko slowed, then stopped. She turned just enough to face them, lantern light catching along the edge of her sleeve.

"Yes," she said. "But we are still here."

The words were simple. They needed nothing added.

The lanterns continued to glow, steady and patient, lighting the path forward without urgency. And for a while longer, the three of them walked on together, letting the moment hold.

Early Morning in Tatsumi

The Starlight Shadow rested in silence beneath the trees, systems idling, canopy dimmed against the rising light. Adrian sat in the pilot's seat with his head tilted back, eyes closed. Not fully asleep. Just balanced between rest and readiness, a habit learned the hard way.

Freija and Kimiko were asleep behind him in the only two bunks the small ship had.

The sound outside tipped that balance.

Footsteps. Too many. Too quick.

Voices followed. Low. Urgent. Uneven.

Adrian's eyes opened.

He leaned forward, fingers brushing the console as external sensors activated just enough to feed him sound. The village was awakening earlier than it should have been. Doors opening. Voices overlapping. A tight edge in the air that had not been there the night before.

"That's not normal," he muttered.

He turned and raised his voice, controlled but firm. "Kimi–"

She was moving before the word finished leaving his mouth.

Kimiko sat up in one smooth motion, already listening. The stillness she carried the night before was gone, replaced by focus. She did not ask what was wrong. She did not need to.

Outside, a voice rose slightly. Not shouting. Strained.

Kimiko swung her legs from the bunk and reached for her gear. The twin katanas settled across her back in practiced, quiet motions.

Freija woke next, lifting her head as the tension reached her. Her wings flexed once before folding tight. She slid from the bunk and secured her ice-forged short swords at her sides. Her expression remained calm, but her eyes were already searching.

"What happened?" she asked.

Adrian stood and moved toward the ramp. "We're about to find out."

The ramp lowered with a soft hiss.

Morning air rushed in, carrying unease with it. Several villagers stood gathered near the path, faces drawn tight. When they saw Kimiko, relief flickered briefly before giving way to worry.

"He has not answered," an elder said. "Master Shigenori did not come at dawn."

Kimiko stepped forward. "Where is he?"

"He should be in his quarters. Near the shrine."

She nodded once. "Take us there."

They moved quickly, but without panic. The village held itself together, as if noise alone might make things worse. Freija walked slightly behind Kimiko, eyes lifting toward rooftops and tree lines. Adrian kept pace on the other side, already mapping routes and angles without conscious effort.

The door to the Master's quarters stood open.

Kimiko stopped.

"That door should be closed," she said quietly.

From where they stood, they could see just enough.

A table lay on its side near the center of the room. The bed beyond it was disturbed, blankets pulled free, the careful order of the space broken in a way that felt abrupt rather than violent.

No one stepped forward.

The elder that led them there let out a quiet gasp in disbelief.

The absence spoke louder than any cry.

Chapter 3:
The Investigation

The Empty Room

Kimiko crossed the threshold first. She did not rush. She did not hesitate.

She slipped into the room as if entering hostile territory, posture low, steps measured. Her eyes moved constantly. Corners. Shadows. The space beneath the bed. The angle of the overturned table. She did not touch anything. She did not need to.

Freija followed more openly, wings folded tight against her back. She moved around the room in a slow, widening arc, taking in details Kimiko might have ignored. Texture. Disturbance. Absence.

Adrian remained just inside the doorway.

He did not step farther in. He didn't need to. His eyes traced the same lines, already cataloging.

Behind them, the elder swallowed hard. "This should not be open," he said quietly.

Kimiko did not look back. "Please notify the others," she said. "Calmly."

The elder nodded once and turned away, moving faster than his years would normally suggest.

Inside, the room spoke volumes.

The table lay overturned near the center, its surface scarred but intact. The Master's bedding was disordered. Blankets dragged free. The mattress shifted as if weight had pressed into it suddenly, then released.

Freija paused near the table.

A broken teacup lay beside it. Porcelain cracked cleanly down one side. A small puddle had soaked into the floorboards, the scent of tea still faintly present.

"There was a struggle," Freija said. "Short."

Kimiko's gaze shifted, following the line of disturbance. From the table. To the doorframe.

A thin strip of fabric clung to a splintered edge of the doorframe. Dark. Woven. Torn, not cut.

Adrian saw it too.

"Hold," he said quietly.

He reached behind his back, pulled out a leather glove, and carefully freed the fabric from the wood. He folded it once and slipped it into his jacket pocket.

"I'll take that back to the ship," he said. "Run a scan and see what it tells us."

Freija crouched near the threshold, careful not to disturb the packed earth outside. "They couldn't have carried him far." she said.

Kimiko straightened slowly.

"This was controlled," she said. "Someone trained. Someone who knew exactly how much force to use."

Footsteps sounded behind them.

A young man in simple ceremonial robes stood frozen in the doorway.

For a moment, he did not move.

His breath caught as his eyes took in the room.

"No," he whispered.

Then, louder, breaking. "No!"

Kimiko turned and immediately recognized the young man. "You brought the Master his lantern last night during the blessing ceremony," she said.

The man nodded sharply. "Yes. My name is Hiroto. I am one of the initiates." His voice tightened. "He did not answer the morning bell. He has never missed it. Not once. Not in over forty years."

Freija watched him closely.

Hiroto's gaze drifted past Kimiko, past the overturned table, and stopped.

The broken teacup.

Color drained from his face.

"I brought him tea last night," he said quietly. "After the ceremony. He always takes it before retiring."

Kimiko was already turning back to him. "What time?"

"Abou... Abou... About eight-thirty," Hiroto said, trembling now. "If it was still full, then whoever took him must have been close. Watching. Waiting for me to leave."

Initiate Hiroto

Silence pressed in around them.

Hiroto was visibly shaking. "The Master," he said. "He is frail. This should not have happened to him. We must find him. Bring him back."

Kimiko met his eyes. "Then we will find him."

Hiroto took a step toward the bed, then stopped. "If he is not returned before dusk..." His voice faltered. "The ceremony cannot proceed."

Kimiko studied him for a brief moment. Not unkindly.

"I am not ready," Hiroto finished quietly.

Freija shifted her focus back outside.

"There's a trail," she said.

Hiroto's head snapped up. "Which way?"

Freija rose to her full height and stepped into the morning light. "East. The trail goes to the East."

Kimiko opened her mouth.

Freija didn't wait.

"I'll follow it," she said. "I'll report back."

Her wings unfolded only once she was clear of the structure. She lifted cleanly into the air, the sun already three-quarters risen, light spilling across the village as she vanished beyond the rooftops.

Silence settled in her wake.

Kimiko turned back to the room.

Adrian's hand rested near the pocket holding the fabric. "This wasn't random," he said.

"No," Kimiko agreed. "It was deliberate."

"Whoever this person is," Adrian said quietly, "they already have quite a bit of a lead."

Outside, the village began to stir. Inside, the investigation had truly begun.

What Remains

The room felt smaller without Freija in it.

Hiroto stood near the wall, hands clasped tightly in front of him. He had not moved since Freija took to the air. His eyes followed the sunlight as it crept across the floor, unfocused, as if searching for something that was no longer there.

Kimiko remained near the center of the room. Not pacing. Not still. Just... present. She let her gaze move once more, slower now, confirming what instinct had already told her.

"They did not come to destroy," she said quietly. "They came to remove."

Hiroto swallowed. "Why him?"

Kimiko met his eyes. "Because he matters."

That answer seemed to land harder than any other.

Adrian stepped back toward the doorway, careful not to disturb the threshold. He withdrew the folded strip of fabric from his jacket pocket and held it up just enough for Kimiko to see.

"This isn't from here," he said. "The weave's wrong. Synthetic blend, but old-tech manufacture. Someone wanted durability, not comfort."

Hiroto looked at it, then away. "So, he planned this."

"Yes," Adrian said. "Which means they didn't panic. And they didn't improvise."

Kimiko nodded once. "And they knew when he would be alone."

Silence settled again.

Outside, voices drifted faintly through the trees. Word was spreading, slowly but steadily. The village was waking into uncertainty.

Kimiko turned to Hiroto. Her voice softened but did not lose its steadiness.

"You did nothing wrong."

He shook his head once. "I should have stayed. I should have noticed something."

"You noticed what mattered," she said. "And you came when something felt wrong. That is not failure."

Hiroto held her gaze for a long moment, then nodded. Just once.

Adrian glanced toward the sky, where Freija had vanished minutes earlier. "She'll confirm direction soon. Once we know where the trail truly goes, we move."

Kimiko's eyes narrowed slightly. "They wanted us looking east."

Adrian raised an eyebrow. "That obvious?"

"It is the direction that feels right," she said. "Which makes it wrong."

A faint, grim smile touched his mouth. "I like how you think."

Kimiko stepped toward the doorway at last, careful to avoid the disturbed earth.

"Close the room," she said. "No one enters until we return."

Hiroto straightened instinctively. "I'll see that it is done."

As they stepped back into the morning light, the village of Tatsumi continued to stir around them. Lanterns swayed gently overhead, unlit now, waiting for a night that might not come as planned.

Above them, somewhere beyond sight, Freija followed a trail already thinning with the day.

And whatever had taken Master Shigenori was counting on time.

Learning of Possible Suspects

The gathering hall stood just beyond the shrine; its doors open to the morning air.

Kimiko removed her sandals before entering, a habit older than memory. Inside, the space was spare and deliberate. Tatami mats worn smooth by generations. Low tables arranged with intention rather than comfort. Scrolls lined the far wall, their ink softened by time and careful hands. This was not a place where answers were demanded. It was where they were allowed to surface.

Three elders sat nearest the center. Two adepts stood behind them, ceremonial sashes draped across their shoulders. All had risen early. All already knew why she had come.

Kimiko bowed first. Deep. Respectful.

"Master Shigenori is missing," she said. "I am not here to accuse. I am here to understand."

One of the elders inclined his head. "Then you ask the correct way."

Adrian remained near the entrance, silent. Present, but deliberately out of the circle.

Kimiko took a single step forward. "Tell me," she said, "who carried resentment toward the Master."

The elders exchanged a glance.

"Resentment takes many forms," one said carefully.

"Yes," Kimiko replied. "That is why I am asking."

Silence stretched. Then one of the adepts spoke.

"There was a foreigner," he said. "A man who came here years ago."

Another elder nodded. "Ah, yes... Olu."

Kimiko did not react. She listened.

"He was not Japanese," the elder continued. "A black man. Nigerian, I believe. Strong. Physically imposing. He believed discipline should answer to strength, not restrain it."

"He challenged the Master openly," an adept added. "Mocked the rites. Called them relics."

"And when he was corrected," the elder said, "he did not accept it."

"He left angry," another said. "Believing something had been taken from him."

Adrian's eyes narrowed slightly, but he said nothing.

Kimiko inclined her head. "He was hostile."

"Yes," the elder said. "If anyone bore anger, it was Olu."

She let that settle.

"Was there anyone else?"

Another pause.

"There was Kenji," one of the adepts said.

Kimiko's gaze shifted. "Tell me."

"Japanese," the adept continued. "A senior student. Skilled. Patient. He never disrespected the Master, but he disagreed with him."

"In what way?" Kimiko asked.

"He believed tradition was being preserved at the cost of progress," the elder said. "That adaptation was being delayed."

"But he never challenged openly," the adept added. "He left quietly."

"Controlled," Adrian murmured, almost to himself.

Kimiko heard him but did not respond.

"And anyone else?" she asked.

The room grew quieter.

"There was one more," an elder said at last. "Yuto."

Kimiko waited.

"He was dismissed early," the elder continued. "Undisciplined. Impatient."

"But not loud," the adept added. "He kept his anger inward."

"He wanted mastery without restraint," the elder said. "But he lacked patience. He did not stay long."

Kimiko considered that.

"Did he threaten the Master?" she asked.

"No," the elder said. "He brooded. He withdrew."

Kimiko nodded slowly.

"So," she said, summarizing without judgment, "one man who left in anger. One who left in disagreement. And one who left quietly, frustrated."

"Yes," the elder said. "Those are the main fractures."

Adrian shifted his stance slightly. "And if you had to guess which one would act first?"

The elders did not answer immediately.

"Olu," one said finally. "If anyone would return violently, it would be him."

"Kenji would be more calculated," another added. "If he acted at all."

"And Yuto?" Kimiko asked.

The elder shook his head. "He lacks the discipline for something like this."

Kimiko absorbed that, but her expression did not change.

"Resentment does not always announce itself the way we expect," she said quietly.

"No," the elder agreed. "But some resentments burn hotter than others."

Kimiko bowed again. "Thank you. This helps."

As she turned toward the doorway, Adrian called out again, "Where are they now?"

Kimiko paused turning to look back at the men.

One of the adepts said, "Olu went north toward Fukui. Kenji went northeast towards Tokyo. And Yuto went south toward Kobe."

Adrian bowed. "Thank you."

Kimiko resumed her pace and joined Adrian.

"So," he said softly, "we've got one obvious candidate, one possible candidate, and one unlikely one."

"For now," Kimiko replied.

Outside, the village continued to stir beneath the rising sun.

What the Evidence Says

Adrian sat at the narrow dining table built into the Starlight Shadow's living area, one forearm resting against its surface as the handheld scanner hummed quietly in his grip.

The torn strip of fabric was held in tweezers in his left hand. Dark. Woven. Ordinary at first glance.

He adjusted the scanner's settings, eyes narrowing as the data stabilized.

"Okay," he said quietly. "That's something."

Kimiko stood nearby, arms folded within her kimono sleeves. She had not sat. She had not leaned. She waited the way she always did, fully present without pressing.

"What do you have?" she asked.

"Dried sweat residue," Adrian replied. "Enough to pull a clean profile. Male. Human. No degradation yet."

Kimiko absorbed that. "So, this is definitely from the man in the room?"

"Yeah." He nodded once. "Whoever took the Master was close enough, long enough, and moving under stress in this August heat."

The ship vibrated faintly.

A shadow crossed the canopy.

The airlock cycled open.

Freija stepped inside, wings folding tight as she closed the hatch. Her expression was focused, her posture grounded. She did not look relieved. She looked restrained.

She glanced between them. "What have you learned?"

Adrian shifted in his seat and glanced toward Kimiko. "Do you want to tell her, or should I?"

Kimiko did not hesitate. "I will."

She turned to Freija. "We spoke with the elders and adepts. We asked who carried resentment toward the Master. Not who was nearby. Who could have reason."

Freija listened without interrupting.

"There are three men," Kimiko continued. "Olu. A foreigner who trained here years ago. Strong. Hostile. He openly challenged the Master and left in anger."

Freija's jaw tightened. "That sounds promising."

"Kenji," Kimiko said, "was a senior student. Japanese. Skilled. He disagreed with the Master's adherence to tradition, but he never disrespected him. He left quietly."

"And the third?" Freija asked.

"Yuto," Kimiko said. "Dismissed early. Undisciplined. Frustrated. He wanted mastery without restraint. But he lacked patience."

Freija considered that. "So, Olu is the most likely?"

"That is what the elders believe," Kimiko replied.

Adrian tapped the scanner lightly against the table. "Which brings us back to this."

Freija's gaze dropped to the device. "And?"

"And at first glance," Adrian said, "it looked like it supported that theory."

Freija's eyes brightened slightly. "You mean he isn't Japanese."

"Hold on," Adrian said. "That was my assumption. Not the conclusion."

He adjusted the scanner again. The hum deepened briefly, then steadied.

Kimiko watched his face, not the screen.

Adrian exhaled slowly.

"No," he said. "That was wrong. Full profile just finished compiling."

Freija stiffened. "Wrong how?"

Adrian looked up. "The DNA is human. Male. And distinctly Japanese."

The silence that followed was immediate.

Kimiko closed her eyes briefly.

"That removes Olu," she said.

"Completely," Adrian confirmed. "He wasn't in that room."

Freija stared at the scanner. "So, it's Kenji."

"He becomes the most likely," Kimiko said. "Based on motive alone."

Adrian nodded. "And location. Olu went north toward Fukui. Kenji went northeast, toward Tokyo. Yuto went south."

Freija's head snapped up. "South!?!!"

"Yes," Adrian said carefully. "Why?"

Freija hesitated, then spoke. "The trail I followed started east. Clean. Deliberate. Whoever it was knew how to mislead."

Kimiko's eyes sharpened. "And then?"

Freija exhaled. "After a while, it went cold. Stone roadway. No soil. No imprint. I lost it."

Adrian leaned back slightly. "And when it resumed?"

Freija looked between them. "It didn't resume. Not east."

Kimiko felt the shift before it was spoken.

Freija continued, slower now. "I circled wider. Lower. Eventually I picked it up again."

Adrian's voice was quiet. "Where?"

Freija swallowed once. "South."

No one spoke.

Outside, Tatsumi continued its uneasy morning. Bells rang softly in the distance. Doors opened. Voices murmured.

Inside the ship, the investigation pivoted.

And somewhere ahead of them, the wrong man had already been crossed off the list.

Chapter 4: The Confrontation

Southern Grounds

The Starlight Shadow skimmed low over the southern terrain, engines dialed back to a steady, controlled hum. Below them, the land shifted from cultivated paths to uneven stone and overgrowth, the geometry of the village giving way to terrain shaped by time rather than maintenance.

Adrian kept his hands light on the controls, eyes moving between the forward canopy and the tactical display. "This is it," he said. "Southern sector. Old training grounds. No recent traffic markers except one narrow approach."

Kimiko sat in the co-pilot's seat, posture straight, gaze fixed on the land ahead. She did not question the choice. She recognized the area the moment it appeared on the display.

"Students who failed discipline were sent there," she said quietly. "Not as punishment. As reflection."

Freija stood near the airlock, wings folded tight against her back. She did not look back. She did not need instruction.

Adrian adjusted altitude and speed with care, bringing the ship into a shallow pass along the edge of the clearing, keeping them outside the open grounds. "I'll keep scanning from here. Life-sign sweep is active."

The airlock cycled open.

Freija stepped forward and dropped cleanly from the ship, body compact, controlled. For a heartbeat she fell in silence, matching the ship's velocity. Then her wings snapped open, catching the air with practiced precision. She angled away from the Starlight Shadow and accelerated along a diverging path, low and fast, eyes already tracking the terrain below.

Adrian watched her signal separate cleanly before returning his focus to the scanners. "You're clear," he said. "I'm picking up something ahead. Weak. Stationary."

Kimiko leaned forward slightly, attention sharpening. "The Master."

Freija flew wide, circling the outer edge of the grounds rather than cutting straight in. Broken stone and moss-covered platforms passed beneath her as she scanned the area from above. Then she saw it.

A figure lay near the remains of a stone structure, partially shielded by fallen beams and overgrowth. Alive. Breathing. Unconscious, but not restrained.

"I see him," Freija said into the comm. "Master Shigenori. He's alive."

Adrian exhaled slowly. "Good. Any sign of movement nearby?"

Freija widened her arc, climbing slightly to gain perspective. "Negative. No one guarding him."

Kimiko closed her eyes for a moment, then opened them again. Relief did not soften her. It focused her.

"He did not intend to kill him," she said. "Not yet."

Freija adjusted her course, preparing to descend. "I'm moving in to secure the Master."

Adrian brought the ship into a holding pattern above the grounds, scanners still active. "Do it carefully. Whoever took him knew this place."

Below them, the abandoned training grounds lay quiet once more. Stone and earth held their secrets close.

The Master had been found.

The one responsible had not.

The Weight of the Light

Freija reached the Master first.

She knelt beside him without hesitation, wings folding tight against her back as her hands hovered briefly before making contact. He was conscious. Shaken. Breathing shallowly, but steady. Relief moved through her like a current, swift and quiet, never softening her alertness.

"You're safe," she said, her voice low and certain. "I will protect you."

Her ice-forged short swords remained sheathed. Her wings loosened instead, unfurling just enough to cast shadow over him, blocking the open sky without announcing threat.

Yuto

Every muscle was engaged. Every sense tuned outward. She positioned herself between the Master and the surrounding trees, body angled slightly forward, ready to absorb the world if it came for him.

The clearing was still.

Then footsteps crunched against gravel.

Freija looked up.

Yuto emerged from the shadows near the broken edge of the old training grounds. His movements were sharp, tense, and trained. He saw Freija first, registered her wings, her petite size, her placement over the Master.

He attacked anyway.

The strike was fast. Desperate. A blade meant to force distance.

Freija intercepted it with a single step and drawing one of her ice-forged blades.

Steel met ice with a sharp crack, her parry clean and effortless. She turned his momentum aside and sent him stumbling backward, her second blade coming up defensively, never chasing, never over committing.

"Enough," she warned.

Yuto froze.

Not because he was afraid of her strength. But because he recognized it.

Before either could move again, the hum of engines faded behind them. The Starlight Shadow settled at the edge of the clearing, landing with practiced ease. The ramp lowered.

Kimiko stepped down first.

She did not draw her katanas.

Her hands were empty as she approached, posture calm, measured. Her eyes moved once, briefly, to the Master, then to Freija. A silent acknowledgment passed between them.

Adrian followed, slower, observant, one hand resting casually near the disruptor in its holder. He took in the scene in a single glance. The Master alive. Freija grounded and ready. Kimiko advancing without threat.

Yuto's breath was uneven now. He shifted his weight, torn between instinct and uncertainty.

"You still don't see it," he said, his voice tight but controlled. "The rite was never meant to become a performance. Lanterns and words and reverence for names carved into wood while the living are told to endure in silence."

His gaze flicked toward the Master, then back to Kimiko.

"He chose memory over truth. Over change. Over those of us who stayed behind when others left. I didn't take him to harm him. I took him because no one listens to students. They only listen when the Master is gone."

Kimiko stopped several paces away.

She did not raise her voice.

"You misunderstand the rite," she said. "It does not bind the living to the past. It reminds them they are not alone as they move forward."

She took one step closer.

"You believe tradition stole your voice. But you never asked what it was trying to teach you." Her head inclined slightly. "Master Shigenori prepares others to carry the light, not replace him. That path was never denied to you."

Yuto moved.

The attack was clumsy this time. Emotional. Predictable.

Kimiko disarmed him in a single motion.

A pivot. A redirect. The weapon struck the ground several steps away, spinning uselessly before coming to rest. She did not strike again. She did not pursue.

She stood there, steady and unyielding.

"You chose force when patience was required," she said quietly. "That is why you were not ready."

Behind her, Adrian exhaled and shook his head faintly.

"For the record," he said, tone dry, "this is exactly why group discussions exist."

Freija, wings still expanded in a protective pose, remained beside the Master, blades sheathed but ready, her body a shield. Only when Kimiko met her gaze did she allow herself to ease slightly, just enough to breathe.

Yuto dropped to his knees.

Not in defeat. In understanding.

The rite had never been taken from him.

He had walked away from it.

And now, surrounded by those who carried it without domination or fear, he finally understood the weight of the light he had tried to steal.

Shared Light

Kimiko helped the Master stand and guided him toward the ship.

She walked beside him with deliberate care, matching her pace to his weakened steps, one hand ready but never grasping unless needed. After a few steps, the master asked her to stop. He turned around to see Yuto still kneeling on the ground in tears.

His gaze settled on Yuto.

"You carried anger where patience was required," he said. "And you mistook silence for rejection."

Yuto's jaw tightened. He did not look away.

"But anger means you still cared," the Master continued. "And that means your path was never closed."

He lifted his hand. Not in judgment. Not in command.

"May you learn to carry light without needing to seize it. May discipline find you before regret does. And may you walk forward without dragging the weight of this moment behind you."

The hand lowered.

Nothing else was said.

Yuto's breath hitched once and he nodded.

When they reached the Starlight Shadow, Kimiko guided him up the ramp and into the cockpit without ceremony or urgency.

"Here," she said gently, helping him settle into the co-pilot's seat.

Master Shigenori nodded, breath shallow but steady. His hands rested on the console.

Kimiko did not sit.

She remained standing near the doorway, posture straight, eyes outward, as if the space itself required her vigilance. She did not need to explain. Adrian understood.

"Securing now," he said quietly as the ship lifted.

Outside, Freija stepped back from the clearing and launched skyward. Her wings fully extended as she flew back toward the village. She arced away from the Shadow and followed a separate path home, a silent sentinel returning on her own terms.

The village came back into view beneath the lowering sun.

When they landed, Initiate Hiroto was already waiting.

He rushed forward the moment the ramp lowered, worry etched deep across his face. He froze briefly when he saw the Master, then moved closer, hands trembling as he knelt.

"You are hurt," he said, voice tight. "I should have been there."

Master Shigenori rested a hand on his shoulder.

"You were," he said quietly. "You simply did not know it yet."

Hiroto swallowed and nodded, tears threatening but held back through sheer will.

The rest of the day passed slowly.

The Master remained conscious but weakened. He spoke little. When he did, it was with effort. By mid-afternoon, he beckoned Hiroto closer.

"The lanterns will be released tonight," he said. "The rite cannot wait for strength to return."

Hiroto stiffened. "Master, I am not prepared."

Shigenori's gaze remained steady. "You are prepared enough. And you will not stand alone."

He reached for Hiroto's hand and held it firmly.

"We will perform the ceremony together."

Silence followed.

Hiroto bowed deeply, forehead nearly touching the floor. "Then I will do my best."

"That," the Master said, "has always been enough."

Chapter 5: The Ceremony

It's Time to Begin

Hiroto's hands would not stop shaking.

He stood at the base of the platform with his head bowed, fingers clenched tightly in the folds of his ceremonial robe, breathing slowly through his nose the way he had been taught.

In... Hold... Out... Again.

The words echoed in his thoughts, but they did little to still the tremor in his arms.

Beside him, Master Shigenori waited.

The staff was in the Master's hand now, its polished surface catching the lantern light as evening settled over the village. He stood straighter than his body truly allowed, shoulders squared through will alone. Age and exhaustion weighed on him, but his presence remained intact.

Hiroto glanced up, just once.

The Master noticed.

"You are thinking too loudly," Shigenori said softly.

Hiroto swallowed. "I am afraid I will fail."

The Master's lips curved, faint but real. "Then you are listening."

He shifted his weight, and Hiroto reacted instantly, stepping forward without being asked. He placed one steady hand near the Master's elbow, careful not to grip unless needed. The staff tapped once against the stone as they began the slow ascent.

Each step was deliberate.

Hiroto matched the pace exactly, adjusting when the Master faltered, anticipating when his breath shortened. When Shigenori paused, Hiroto paused. When he leaned, Hiroto absorbed the weight without comment. No one watching could tell where guidance ended and assistance began.

That was the point.

They reached the platform.

The Master's breathing had grown shallow. He rested the staff against the wood and closed his eyes briefly. Hiroto waited, unmoving, until the Master nodded once.

"Sit," Shigenori said.

Hiroto guided him to the low ceremonial seat, then knelt beside him, head bowed, waiting for instruction.

"You will begin," the Master said. "Read."

Hiroto's heart stuttered.

He reached for the scroll with careful hands, unrolling it across the stand the way he had practiced countless times alone. The paper whispered softly in the night air. He cleared his throat once, then began, voice low but steady, carrying.

"We gather not to release what is lost," he read, "but to remember what remains."

The words settled into the space.

Nearby, the stream reflected lantern light in broken ribbons of gold. Villagers stood along its edge in respectful silence. Children were held close. Elders leaned on canes worn smooth by years of patience. No one spoke.

A short distance away, the trio watched.

Freija stood with her wings folded tight, hands clasped loosely in front of her. Kimiko remained perfectly still, eyes forward, posture reverent. Adrian stood silent with arms crossed, expression unreadable.

Hiroto continued.

When the Master lifted his hand, Hiroto stopped instantly.

Shigenori opened his eyes and looked out over the gathering. His voice, when he spoke, was weaker than usual, but no less certain.

"The light we release tonight does not belong to us," he said. "It belongs to those who came before, and those who will come after."

Hiroto bowed his head, tears blurring the ink on the scroll. He blinked them away and resumed reading.

The ceremony had begun.

And for the first time, Hiroto understood that he was not carrying it alone.

The Trio's Release

The sky deepened from indigo to near black, stars faint but present above the village rooftops. Along the riverbank, lanterns drifted in slow, deliberate currents, their colors spread softly across the water. Warm golds. Deep crimson. Muted greens. Violet. Each hue was chosen with intention, each flame steady within its paper shell.

The festival had begun.

Kimiko knelt at the edge of a narrow wooden dock, the water close enough that she could hear it move. In her hands rested a single lantern, its paper dyed a calm ivory with delicate inked lines along the frame. The candle inside waited, unlit.

Behind her, the sounds of the village carried quietly. Murmured voices. A distant drum, slower now. Not celebration. Continuation.

Freija and Adrian approached without speaking. Their footsteps softened as they reached the dock, both instinctively aware that this moment did not belong to noise.

Kimiko looked up at them, her expression composed, but lighter than it had been earlier that day.

"Thank you," she said, "for bringing me here."

Adrian gave a small shrug. "After everything that happened, it felt right to see this through."

Freija nodded, wings folded close, her gaze drawn to the lanterns moving across the river. "They are beautiful," she said. "Each one feels different."

"They are," Kimiko replied. "The colors carry meaning. Red for gratitude. Gold for guidance. Green for renewal. White for remembrance." She lowered her eyes to the lantern in her hands. "Not rules. Intentions."

She struck a slender match and touched it to the wick. The flame caught gently, illuminating her fingers with soft light. She did not speak at first.

"This one," Kimiko said at last, "is for those who gave me my first understanding of discipline. Of silence. Of purpose."

She lowered her gaze to the lantern.

"For my parents. For what they taught without ever needing to name it."

The light wavered once.

A single tear slipped free, tracking silently along her cheek before falling into the river below. Kimiko did not wipe it away. She did not break her posture.

"And for Master Shigenori," she continued, her voice unchanged, "for carrying that same light forward. For patience. For teaching without asking to be remembered. And for the strength he showed today, even when his body could not keep pace with his spirit."

She set the lantern onto the water.

It drifted slowly away its ivory glow steady as it followed the current.

Freija hesitated. A lantern lay nearby, its paper shell catching the river light.

"Is it permitted?" she asked quietly. "For someone like me?"

Kimiko met her gaze and nodded. "That is why I asked you to come."

Freija lowered herself to one knee beside her. The lantern she lifted was pale gold, its surface brushed with subtle geometric patterns. She lit it carefully, as if afraid of disturbing something unseen.

"I release mine," she said, voice quiet but clear, "for the places that shaped me. For the sister who still walks beside me, even when she is far away. And for the warmth I have found beyond the cold I once believed defined me."

Her breath caught briefly, then steadied.

She placed the lantern on the water and watched it drift until it aligned with Kimiko's.

Adrian hesitated before stepping forward. His lantern was a deep red, unadorned, its color rich without flourish. He lit it in silence, holding it a moment longer than necessary.

"This one is for the people I did not save," he said. "And for the choices I am still learning to make better." He glanced toward the river. "And for the improbable fact that I am still here. With both of you."

He set the lantern down.

The three lights moved together. Not bound, but close enough to matter.

The stream carried them onward, their reflections stretching and narrowing as they rounded the bend, joining the countless others already moving toward the dark.

Freija reached out, resting her hand lightly against Kimiko's shoulder. Adrian stood just beside them watching the drift of the lanterns.

THE NIGHT OF A THOUSAND LANTERNS: A LESSON OF RELEASE

For a time, none of them spoke.
The lanterns drifted on.
And in their wake, the night held.

Epilogue: The Light That Remains

The Master's chambers were quiet in the way that follows survival.

Late afternoon light filtered through the paper screens, softened by age and time. Outside, the village had resumed its rhythm. Footsteps passed. Wind stirred the bamboo. Somewhere beyond the walls, water moved steadily along its course. The world had not stopped. It had waited.

A single lantern rested on a low wooden table near the window.

Its paper was cream-colored, unadorned except for a few simple brushstrokes. The flame inside burned steadily. Not bright. Not dim. It did not demand attention. It simply remained.

Hiroto stood at the entrance to the room, hands folded, shoulders straight but tense. He had been summoned, yet he did not step forward until invited. He had learned, through fear and failure alike, that presence was as much about restraint as action.

Master Shigenori sat opposite the lantern.

He was thinner now. Recovery had not restored what had been taken. But his back was straight, his gaze clear. His staff rested against the wall nearby, within reach but unused.

"You may come in," the Master said.

Hiroto bowed deeply before stepping forward. He knelt where indicated, eyes lowered, breath controlled but uneven. The days since the ceremony had passed in a blur. Relief. Guilt. Gratitude. All of it tangled together.

Shigenori studied him for a long moment.

Not as a Master judging an Initiate. As a teacher observing what had endured.

"You were afraid," the Master said at last.

Hiroto did not hesitate. "Yes."

"You doubted yourself."

"Yes."

"You believed you were not ready."

Hiroto's hands tightened slightly against his robes. "I still believe that."

A faint smile touched the Master's mouth. Not amusement. Recognition.

"Good," Shigenori said.

Hiroto looked up, startled.

"Those who believe themselves ready too soon are the ones who fail the rite," the Master continued. "Readiness is not certainty. It is responsibility accepted in uncertainty."

He reached toward the table, not for the lantern, but for a small bundle resting beside it.

The wrapping was simple. Rice paper, folded with care. No markings. No seal.

"You carried the space when I could not," the Master said. "And you did so without seeking to be seen."

He extended the bundle toward Hiroto.

"This is for you."

Hiroto hesitated, then accepted it with both hands. The paper was soft beneath his fingers. Light, but not empty.

"Open it," Shigenori said.

Carefully, Hiroto unfolded the rice paper.

Inside lay fabric folded and worn. A ceremonial sash.

The fabric was familiar. Worn at the edges. Not decorative, but purposeful. A piece that had been earned, not displayed.

Hiroto's breath caught.

"I do not give this lightly," the Master said. "It is not a reward. It is a responsibility."

Hiroto lowered his head, emotion pressing hard against his chest.

"When you stood beside me at dusk," Shigenori continued, "your voice trembled. Your hands did not. You listened. You waited. You honored the silence as much as the words."

He paused.

"You carried the rite forward without trying to claim it."

Hiroto's vision blurred. He bowed deeply, forehead nearly touching the floor.

"I only followed what you taught me," he said quietly. "What you lived."

Shigenori inclined his head. "And in doing so, you showed me something important."

He rested his hand briefly against the table.

"You showed me that the light does not depend on strength alone."

The room was still.

"From this day forward," the Master said, his voice calm and certain, "you are no longer an Initiate."

The words did not rush. They did not need to.

"You are an Adept of the Lantern Rite."

Hiroto remained kneeling, the sash cradled in his hands.

Emotion rose in him, sharp and unguarded. Pride, yes. But also fear. And humility. And the weight of knowing that advancement was not an end, but a beginning.

"I accept," he said, voice steady despite the tears he no longer tried to hide. "With gratitude. With responsibility. And with the understanding that I still have much to learn."

The Master's eyes softened.

"That," he said quietly, "is why you are ready."

They sat together for a while longer, the lantern flame unwavering between them.

At last, Hiroto rose. He placed the sash around his neck. He bowed once more before turning to leave.

After the door slid shut, the Master gave a single, confident nod. A small smile followed.

About the Author

K.A. Dunlap is a science fiction author and worldbuilder exploring the quieter moments that shape extraordinary lives. While the Crimson Alliance Universe is known for its epic conflicts and formidable heroes, *Thousand Lanterns* reflects a different side of that universe – one rooted in reflection, tradition, and the bonds formed between unlikely companions.

Dunlap's stories often examine discipline, identity, and the cost of growth, balancing action with moments of stillness where meaning is found not in victory, but in understanding. He believes that some of the most important stories happen between battles... in conversations, rituals, and choices made when no one is watching.

Thousand Lanterns serves as a gateway into the Crimson Alliance Universe, welcoming new readers while offering longtime fans a deeper look at the values that bind its characters together.

When not writing, K.A. Dunlap enjoys thoughtful storytelling across science fiction and fantasy, and continues to expand the Crimson Alliance Universe through novels, tales, and character-driven side stories.

To learn more about the Crimson Alliance Universe, visit: **https://www.TheCAU.net**

Contact: **KADunlap@TheCAU.net**

Other Stories in the Crimson Alliance Universe

If you enjoyed *The Night of a Thousand Lanterns*, there are other stories waiting for you in the Crimson Alliance Universe (CAU). Each explores a different tone, character, and corner of the galaxy... from epic rebellion to quiet, character-driven journeys.

Stories in the CAU are told at different scales, each chosen to match the moment being explored.

Ensemble Novels

(full cast collection of many or all of the main characters)

A Demon's Rebellion: The Rise of Lilith

Starring: The full Crimson Alliance

This is where it all begins. Follow the formation of the Crimson Alliance as disparate warriors are drawn together to challenge a tyrant whose reach spans worlds. Action-driven, emotional, and character-focused, this novel establishes the heart of the universe.

Genre: Sci-fic opera, humor, drama, emotional intrigue

Interludes

(shorter novels involving one or more main characters)

Sunlight and Shorelines: This Was Supposed to Be a Vacation

Starring: Adrian & Grilka

A luxury couples-only resort. A fake honeymoon. And a conspiracy hiding beneath paradise. Adrian and Grilka's attempt at rest turns into an espionage-laced mystery involving surveillance, identity theft, and secrets buried beneath perfection.

Genre: Sci-fi espionage, humor, character-driven suspense

Cold Front: Echoes in the Frost

Starring: Kimiko, Freija, and Frigid

THE NIGHT OF A THOUSAND LANTERNS: A LESSON OF RELEASE

A trip to Freija's homeworld of Icelandia for Kimiko turns into a world-shattering epic involving Freija's twin sister Frigid and the past is now coming back to bring the world to its knees.

Genre: Sci-fi, character-driven suspense, emotional intrigue

Tales

(10-chapter story arcs involving minor and major characters)

Smuggler's Gambit: Where the Skills End and the Luck Begins

Starring: Adrian, Rafe Juno, and Kevan Dralis

Before alliances were forged, Adrian survived by wit, luck, and bad decisions. This tale dives into the smuggler's underworld and the choices that shaped the pilot he would later become.

Genre: Sci-fi adventure, outlaw drama, sharp humor

The Tournament of Snowfall: The Evolution of a Princess

Starring: Frigid

Set on the frozen world of Icelandia, this tale follows Frigid as she enters a brutal tournament that tests not only her strength, but her understanding of leadership, legacy, and self-worth.

Genre: Warrior fantasy, coming-of-age, cultural tradition

Micro-Tales

(5-chapter story arcs that tell a very short story that still has meaning)

The Night of a Thousand Lanterns: A Lesson of Release

Starring: Kimiko, Freija, and Adrian

A short story where the trio of characters return to Earth to take part in a Japanese ritual of release and remembrance, only to have the ceremony disrupted by someone who does not respect it.

Genre: Science fiction, character-driven, cultural reflection

The Crimson Alliance Universe contains both epic conflicts and intimate stories – because not every moment that shapes a hero happens on a battlefield.

To explore more, visit: **https://www.TheCAU.net**

www.ingramcontent.com/pod-product-compliance
Lightning Source LLC
LaVergne TN
LVHW010945110826
845149LV00013B/2755
9798992981995